Jake an[d]
and the
Castle of Kings

Written by Chris Bradford

Illustrated by Korky Paul

Collins

"Where's my brother?" cried Jake Jones, king of the castle.

"Your majesty, the enemy has captured him!"
replied Jen, his brave fighter.

Jen pointed to a strange lady in white robes. She had put the king's brother in a ditch. Only his head was visible above the sand.

"Save him!" ordered Jake.

"Yes, your majesty," Jen replied. She fetched her horse and spear.

Jake lowered the drawbridge and Jen rode out to do battle.

But a giant was fighting for the enemy. He was the size of a tree and weighed the same as eight elephants.

Jen pulled the reins as her horse neighed in fright.
Jen had to be brave.

"Give me the king's brother, or else!" she shouted.

The giant chuckled. "Or else what?"

"I'll challenge you to a match," said Jen.
"If I win, you free him."

"And if I win ... I put you and your horse in a pie, for lunch!" said the giant, licking his lips.

"That's horrible!" said Jake from the battlements.

The giant rubbed his belly. "And I'll have *you* with jelly for pudding!"

"No, you won't!" said Jen, riding into battle.
"Prepare to die!"

But the giant easily dodged away.

Jen whirled around to try again. This time she was able to nudge him a little.

The giant scratched his belly.
"How feeble!" he yawned.

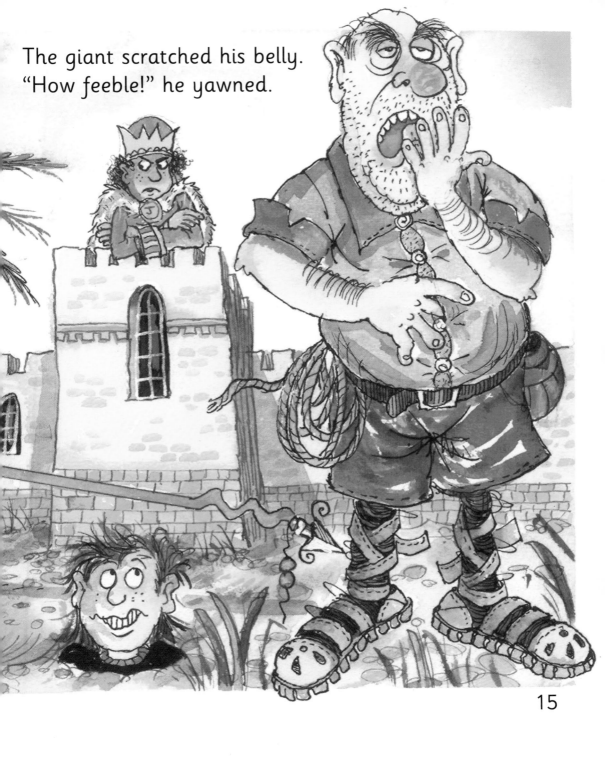

This made Jen angry. She stood on her saddle and charged as hard as she could.

The spear whacked the giant in the stomach.

Whimpering, the giant clutched his aching belly.

He stumbled and fell on the castle. His weight broke the battlements.

"Daddy!" cried Jake. "You have ruined our castle!"

"And scared my donkey!" said Jen.

"Will someone *please* pull me out?" begged their brother.

But their mother just giggled and took a photo!

21

23

🐾 After reading 🐾

Letters and Sounds: Phase 5

Word count: 300

Focus phonemes: /ai/ a, eigh /ee/ e, y, ey /oo/ u /igh/ ie, y /ch/ tch, t /c/ ch /j/ g, ge, dge /l/ le /f/ ph /w/ wh /v/ ve /s/ se /z/ se

Common exception words: of, to, the, into, said, do, someone, our, their

Curriculum links: History

National Curriculum learning objectives: Reading/word reading: apply phonic knowledge and skills as the route to decode words, read other words of more than one syllable that contain taught GPCs; Reading/comprehension: drawing on what they already know or on background information and vocabulary provided by the teacher

Developing fluency

- Your child may enjoy hearing you read the book.
- Take turns to read a page of text. Check that your child uses different voices for the characters and notices the exclamation marks in order to add emphasis to these sentences.

Phonic practice

- Focus on /j/ and /c/ sounds. Ask your child to read the following and identify which contain the /j/ sound:

  strange   fighting   fetched   give   giant   king   drawbridge

- Which of the following contain the /c/ sound?

  scratched   aching   chuckled   ditch   stomach   whacked

Extending vocabulary

- Ask your child to suggest antonyms (opposites) for each of the following:

  brave (e.g. *cowardly, timid*)   horrible (e.g. *lovely, sweet*)
  angry (e.g. *caring, calm*)   feeble (e.g. *strong, powerful*)

- Ask your child to look at the giant on page 6 and think of nice words that one of the giant's friends might choose to describe him. (e.g. *friendly, brave, funny*)